For a united world ...
Britta

CATERPILLAR BOOKS

An imprint of Little Tiger Group

1 The Coda Centre, 189 Munster Road, London SW6 6AW

www.littletiger.co.uk • First published in Great Britain 2017

Text and illustrations copyright © Britta Teckentrup 2017

All rights reserved • ISBN: 978-1-84857-586-8

Printed in China • CPB/1800/0592/0117

10 9 8 7 6 5 4 3 2 1

Under the Same Sky

by Britta Teckentrup

*We live under
the same sky ...*

*... in lands
near and far.*

... *wherever*
we are.

... *in the cold ice*
and snow.

*We feel
the same
love ...*

*... where soft
meadows grow.*

*We play the
same games ...*

... *where the hills touch the sky.*

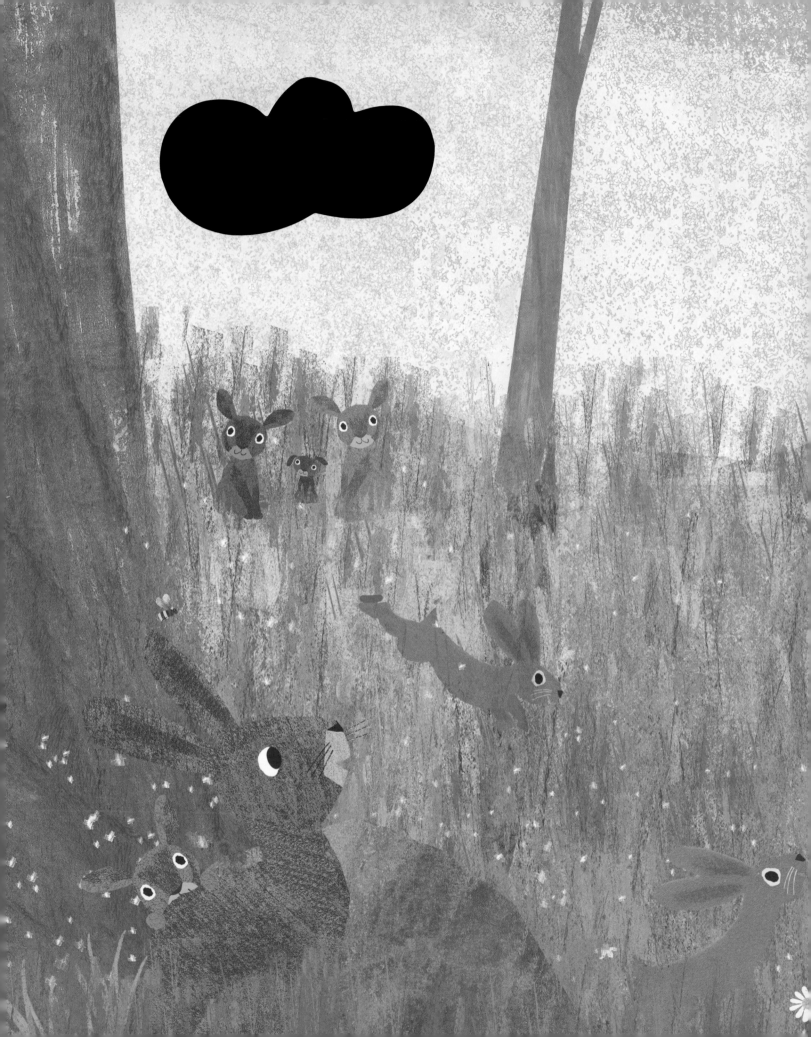

... *where the grass grows so high.*

*We sing the
same songs ...*

*... across the
same seas.*

... *caught on*
the breeze.

...

where
dark
forests
grow.

We

face

the

same

storms

...

...

where

wild

rivers

flow.

... whatever
the weather.

We dream
the same dreams …

and we dream them …

… together.